CORONA
IN THE CITY

Gaithuan Gonmei

WESTBOW
PRESS®
A DIVISION OF THOMAS NELSON
& ZONDERVAN

WestBow Press books may be ordered through booksellers or by contacting:

WestBow Press
A Division of Thomas Nelson & Zondervan
1663 Liberty Drive
Bloomington, IN 47403
www.westbowpress.com
844-714-3454

Scripture marked (KJV) taken from the King James Version of the Bible.

Interior Image Credit: Gaithuan Gonmei

ISBN: 978-1-6642-0175-0 (sc)
ISBN: 978-1-6642-0176-7 (e)

Library of Congress Control Number: 2020915128

Print information available on the last page.

WestBow Press rev. date: 11/04/2020

To the Giver of all good things

CONTENTS

PREFACE

Once in a while, something happens on a global scale which upends life and living as we know it. In such a time, the fragility of the breath of life becomes glaringly apparent and the intricacy of the world we live in is revealed. Placed in different situations, everyone has a distinctive story and as we listen deeply, we expand our consciousness and learn to identify with each other's pain. So often, it is in pain and brokenness that we become willing to dwell upon life and meaning, to think about time and eternity, and to turn to God who created both our hearts and the stars. Our hearts filled with earthly pain may seem to be in stark contrast with the stars filled with ethereal beauty, yet it is we who are the cynosure of the Creator's eyes. In the midst of our fleeting days and short life stories, He beckons us in love to a beautiful life. As in ancient times, the touch of heaven is still available today for those who believe.

1

PAIN AND BEAUTY

He could not find lilies to lay at his beloved's coffin as the death toll mounted beyond the city's ability to cope. And he cried, "As I lay you down with no lilies, I hope it's not too cold down there. I hope your spirit soars and sees beauty."

He did let her go. But his heart was a tangled mess of grief.

"Where your beauty once was in my heart, I now find pain—searing, tearing, blearing pain!"

He cried through the long forlorn hours.
He cried for her. He cried for the beauty that was gone.
He cried because of his pain.
He cried in despair.
He cried.

He peered through the blinds. All he could see were the city lights that shone in cold display deep in the night. Concrete blocks that could not feel his sorrow stared blankly at him. He was oppressed, oppressed by the absence of beauty.

He heard the ambulance screech by in the streets. The blaring siren only made the awareness of his pain more acute. The cacophony outside made a mockery of the melancholy within him.

He writhed in pain. Devoid of consolation, his thoughts turned inwards. He espied memories of days that were and dreams of days that now would never be. Transience taunted him.

With waddled gait, he wandered mindlessly in the barrenness of despondency. Every breath a sigh, he groped in the dark for an undefinable something. He lived in muffled sniffs.

Then something broke one quiet March afternoon. He heard nothing audible, but he was doubly sure it was his heart cracking open. Something came through. And it stirred him.

Could it be that he was open to hear from heaven at long last?

He listened through the cracks in his heart.
He listened for her Lord. He listened for what she would have said.
He listened because of his brokenness.
He listened in hope.
He listened.

He listened to what his open Bible was saying. His tear-stained eyes fell on the verse, "Behold, I make all things new."[1] His glistening tears, through which his pain seeped through, cleared his eyes. With sharper *vision*, he could hear clearer. Having heard, faith[2] arose in his heart. In his grief, he staggered over to the Person who promises to make all things new and he reposed his faith in Him.

---

[1] And he that sat upon the throne said, Behold, I make all things new. And he said unto me, Write: for these words are true and faithful. (Revelation 21:5, KJV)

[2] So then faith cometh by hearing, and hearing by the word of God. (Romans 10:17, KJV). Now faith is the substance of things hoped for, the evidence of things not seen. (Hebrews 11:1, KJV)

The wind blew softly through the curtains as if to celebrate his faith. He gazed out of the window and saw the colours of spring in a vividness he recognised for the first time. As he stood there gazing at the beauteous sight, still pining for his beloved, it was almost as if she whispered through the blowing wind, "Those who understand pain understands beauty. Your pain and His promise equals beauty. You will see me again where all things are made new. Now, go live!"

Those who understand pain understands
beauty. Those who understand pain understands beauty. Those who understand pain
understands beauty. Those who understand
pain understands beauty. Those who understand pain understands beauty. Those who
understand pain understands beauty. Those
who understand pain understands beauty.

**Those who understand pain
understands beauty.** Those who
understand pain understands beauty. Those
who understand pain understands beauty.
Those who understand pain understands
beauty. Those who understand pain understands beauty. Those who understand pain
understands beauty. Those who understand
pain understands beauty. Those who understand pain understands beauty. Those who
understand pain understands beauty. Those

Pain and Beauty

2

MAMA'S TEARS

What shall I do with your lovely dresses? Or your big brown teddy bear? What about your shiny red Mary-Jane shoes that you adore? And your connect-the-dots books and Crayola? Mama sure can treasure them for as long as time lasts, I only ask to know if I may get an inkling of your wish for them.

At five, you were too young to write a will.
After all, little girls are not meant to write wills—
They are meant to dream,
And live and laugh and love.

My girl, you have scattered your magical spark everywhere your little feet have trodden. You have released your sweet presence as from a magical bottle, and Mama will not be able to unbottle it.

Oh, sweet child, how can I forget? I carried you for nine hopeful months to behold your face and hold you tenderly in my arms.

I chose life for you—
So you may see for yourself the beauty that is in the world;
So you may know the song of sparrows and the earthy appeal of petrichor;
So you may participate in the magic of loving, caring, and giving;
So you may taste and see that the Lord is good;[3]
So you may experience my love for you.

---

[3] O taste and see that the Lord is good: blessed is the man that trusteth in him. (Psalm 34:8, KJV)

I imagined a world of love and laughter for you—a world where the country and city mesh in majestic splendour like a sunshower; a world where you are both a sweetheart and a braveheart. But the unimaginable broke in and interrupted the sweet life we lived. Had the malady come negotiating, Mama would have braced it in your stead. But it was invisible. And it was quick. Mama still cannot trace where it all began and took hold of you so swiftly. I wept to see you fighting for dear life on a ventilator.

Your twenty-three thousand breaths a day slowed and slowed to a zero,
Until you slipped away—
Away from mama!

I laid you down to rest tucked in your favourite Elsa quilt blanket, humming "Swing Low, Sweet Chariot"[4] through my tears and trembling lips. And as I held you in my arms for one last time, as I beheld your face for one last time, I mustered all the strength within me to whisper a prayer for me and for you—for God to help me let you go, and for God to hold you in His everlasting arms.[5]

---

[4] An African-American spiritual song written by Wallace Willis

[5] The eternal God is thy refuge, and underneath are the everlasting arms. (Deuteronomy 33:27a, KJV)

So, sweet child of mine—
Sleep, sleep in heavenly peace;
Drift, drift into eternity.
Mama will soon be home with you
To connect, connect the dots together.
Perhaps I will keep your connect-the-dots book for then!

After all, little girls are not meant to write wills—they are meant to dream, and live and laugh and love. After all, little girls are not meant to write wills—they are meant to dream, and live and laugh and love. After all, little girls are not meant to write wills—they are meant to dream, and live and laugh and love. **After all, little girls are not meant to write wills—they are meant to dream, and live and laugh and love.** After all, little girls are not meant to write wills—they are meant to dream, and live and laugh and love. After all, little girls are not meant to write wills—they are meant to dream, and live and laugh and love. After all, little girls are not meant to write wills—they are meant to dream, and live and laugh and love. After all, little girls are not meant to write wills—they are meant to dream, and live and laugh and love.

Mama's Tears

3

GRANDMOTHER AWAITS

I have waited through the winter
To see my dimpled darlin' come home,
From across the seas, from over yonder.
Oh, to see my dimpled darlin' again!

But alas, the world is spinning in a tizzy with an unusual
kind of war, like nothing I have lived through as a child.
I count the thousands of miles between her and me; I

reckon the dwindling time of my golden years. Perhaps we will meet, perhaps not.

So, if I go, will you tell her—
Oh, will you please tell her?
Nev'r to bear the guilt of an unsaid goodbye;
But to know there's a glad reunion across Jordan.
Ah, she is made for such a time as this![6]

I have been to many places over the decades—nothing is quite as sweet as home and home often is not a place but a person.

So, if I go, will you tell her—
Oh, will you please tell her?
Nev'r to forget to come home;
And to choose that one thing which is needful.[7]
Ah, she is made for such a time as this!

I have seen many faces—but no countenance so comely as moulded by contentment, none so misshapen as marked with envy.

So, if I go, will you tell her—
Oh, will you please tell her?

---

[6] And who knoweth whether thou art come to the kingdom for such a time as this? (Esther 4:14b, KJV)

[7] But one thing is needful: and Mary hath chosen that good part, which shall not be taken away from her. (Luke 10:42, KJV)

Nev'r to neglect to work with willing hands;[8]
And to be content yet not complacent.
Ah, she is made for such a time as this!

I have met both poverty and plenty through the years—
truly, we brought nothing into the world and can take
nothing out of it.[9]

So, if I go, will you tell her—
Oh, will you please tell her?
Nev'r to forget to be rich toward God;[10]
And to remember that trust is a currency.
Ah, she is made for such a time as this!

I have never seen the righteous forsaken[11] in all these
years of mine—sometimes slowly, but always surely, the
ancient laws of the universe take their course.

So, if I go, will you tell her—
Oh, will you please tell her?
Nev'r to omit the unseen forces acting in her favour;

---

[8] She seeketh wool, and flax, and worketh willingly with her hands.
(Proverbs 31:13, KJV)

[9] For we brought nothing into this world, and it is certain we can carry
nothing out. (1 Timothy 6:7, KJV)

[10] So is he that layeth up treasure for himself, and is not rich toward God.
(Luke 12:21, KJV)

[11] I have been young, and now am old; yet have I not seen the righteous
forsaken, nor his seed begging bread. (Psalm 37:25, KJV)

And to make it her ambition to live a quiet life.[12]
Ah, she is made for such a time as this!

I have lived a full life—I have known the companionship
of kindred spirits and the help that comes when I lift up
my eyes to the hills.[13]

So, if I go, will you tell her—
Oh, will you please tell her?
Nev'r to feel orphaned in a wild wide world;
But to walk humbly with her big God.[14]
Ah, she sure is made for such a time as this!

Oh, to see my dimpled darlin' again!

---

[12] And that ye study to be quiet, and to do your own business, and to work with your own hands, as we commanded you. (1 Thessalonians 4:11, KJV)
[13] I will lift up mine eyes unto the hills, from whence cometh my help. My help cometh from the Lord, which made heaven and earth. (Psalm 121:1-2, KJV)
[14] He hath shewed thee, O man, what is good; and what doth the Lord require of thee, but to do justly, and to love mercy, and to walk humbly with thy God? (Micah 6:8, KJV)

Nothing is quite as sweet as home and home often is not a place but a person. Nothing is quite as sweet as home and home often is not a place but a person. Nothing is quite as sweet as home and home often is not a place but a person. Nothing is quite as sweet as home and home often is not a place but a person. Nothing is quite as sweet as home and home often is not a place but a person. **Nothing is quite as sweet as home and home often is not a place but a person.** Nothing is quite as sweet as home and home often is not a place but a person. Nothing is quite as sweet as home and home often is not a place but a person. Nothing is quite as sweet as home and home often is not a place but a person. Nothing is quite as sweet as home and home often is not a place but a person. Nothing is quite as sweet as home and

Grandmother Awaits

4

MY HOME ON HIGH

I trudged through the empty avenues and streets. I felt like a king in the square, having the vast expanse all to myself. Those who had comforts were confined indoors with supplies for sustenance. My pockets were empty and I was out in the open with nothing to lose, and how I felt the tall city was my kingdom! Not a dollar in my pocket, I trudged on.

None gave me company except a mouse that scampered by;
Nothing stirred except for my hunger pangs.

The bright warm spring day wore on and dusk settled in with a temperature whiplash. The wet windy evening cut through my threadbare clothes. Damped but not drenched, I began the long walk to the nearest metro station. The station wore a deserted look and I stood at the entrance with no ticket. After a while, a construction worker with his accoutrements exited and he helped me in. I thanked him and walked towards the platform unsure which train to wait for. Not a dollar in my pocket, I waited on.

None spoke except the vapid automated voice on the PA system;
Nothing stirred except for the approaching train.

With nowhere to reach and everywhere to go, I boarded the first train that stopped by and settled down on a two-seater in the corner. The coach was empty and my wandering eyes led me to the *Poetry in Motion*—an owl sat perched on a tree on the yellow poster.[15] The poem and the colour yellow afforded me a sense of hope and optimism. Not a dollar in my pocket, I hoped on.

---

[15] Sze, Arthur. "The Owl." Poetry in Motion by MTA New York City Transit.

None invaded my thoughts except the journeying boy
from *Midnight on the Great Western*;[16]
Nothing stirred except for my heartbeat.

Tattered and tired, I wished for a bowl of hot chicken
soup. I wished for a bar of soap and hot bath. I wished for
a warm cosy bed. I wished for the comforts of home. And
I wished for a heartening story. But my fondest wish of
all was to slip into eternity that night and, like Lazarus,
be comforted in the bosom of Abraham.[17] Through my
whirls of wishes, I drifted off into sleep. Not a dollar in
my pocket, I slept on.

None offered me a shelter except an angel in my dreams
who ushered me to my home on high;
Nothing stirred except for my lilting hallelujah.

I awoke, I awoke to the tapping on my shoulders.
Dreamily, I opened my eyes and looked up. Standing
there was a woman in uniform. She said nothing, her
eyes only gleamed through her masked face. She then
extended her hands to offer me a food parcel flavoured
with an uncommon kindness. Famished, I simply
nodded and took the parcel. I was busy chomping on
the food when the train halted at the boulevard. She

---

[16] Hardy, Thomas. "Midnight on the Great Western." Thomas Hardy:
Selected Poems, Penguin, 1998, p. 136.

[17] And it came to pass, that the beggar died, and was carried by the angels
into Abraham's bosom. (Luke 16:22a, KJV)

arose from her seat, quietly placed her purple cashmere shawl in the vacant seat next to me, and saved me from the awkwardness of words.

The train doors shut tight behind her. She disappeared into the night. I was full and robed in purple. And I found she had fed me with a hearty dose of hope. Not a dollar in my pocket, I travelled on.

I was full and robed in purple. And I found she had fed me with a hearty dose of hope. I was full and robed in purple. And I found she had fed me with a hearty dose of hope. I was full and robed in purple. And I found she had fed me with a hearty dose of hope. I was full and robed in purple. And I found she had fed me with a hearty dose of hope. **I was full and robed in purple. And I found she had fed me with a hearty dose of hope.** I was full and robed in purple. And I found she had fed me with a hearty dose of hope. I was full and robed in purple. And I found she had fed me with a hearty dose of hope. I was full and robed in purple. And I found she had fed me with a hearty dose of hope. I was full and robed in purple. And I found she had fed me with a hearty dose of hope. I was full and robed in purple. And I

My Home on High

5

HEALING BALM OF GILEAD

Wasn't it just a few days ago that life seemed like a long summer song laced with mirth and merriment? I counted it my chief pleasure to trot the globe and hobnob with the who's who. But where I've been, what I've done, and who I've known meant nothing when my life was ebbing away in solitary confinement.

Been there, done that,
But I am undone;

And I need healing—
The Healing Balm of Gilead.[18]

For long, I relied on myself. I banked on my net worth. I counted on my network. I enjoyed the front row. I had the best of what money could buy. Even so, everything evanesced into nothingness with the virulent visitation. The grip of the virus was suffocating, and I gasped for breath. In my solitary struggle, I grasped the fragility of life and the complexity of a simple b-r-e-a-t-h.

Been there, done that,
But I am undone;
And I need healing—
The Healing Balm of Gilead.

Life was upended. All play ceased. Pleasures and profits parted ways with me. As I descended into ventilator limbo, I felt delirious. A different kind of delirium unlike the ones induced by intoxication confronted me. I sensed death. "Go away", I protested with every fibre of my being. But it was a different kind of powerplay, unlike the ones in the boardroom where I held sway.

Been there, done that,
But I am undone;

[18] Is there no balm in Gilead; is there no physician there? why then is not the health of the daughter of my people recovered? (Jeremiah 8:22, KJV)

And I need healing—
The Healing Balm of Gilead.

One moment, I was rolling in luxury and then in the next, as in the twinkling of an eye, I was reeling in fear of being rolled out in a body bag. Over the years, I had burned my body system with alcohol and plagued my immune system with substances. As the reality of death accosted me, I desperately wanted my weakened body mechanism to fight for me. I wanted to be unstrapped from my addictions. I yearned to be healed and made whole.

Been there, done that,
But I am undone;
And I need healing—
The Healing Balm of Gilead.

I had scoffed at the faith that was passed down to me. I knew my mother's faith, but I never knew it for myself. I did not realise that life does not consist in the abundance of things.[19] I thought I was free only to realise how enslaved I was by my own unbelief and the stuffs I *owned*. As I lay on my sick bed, I realised God reigns sovereignly in love and righteousness, neither trespassing my will nor bending to my ways.

---

[19] And he said unto them, Take heed, and beware of covetousness: for a man's life consisteth not in the abundance of the things which he possesseth. (Luke 12:15, KJV)

Been there, done that,
But I am undone;
And I need healing—
The Healing Balm of Gilead.

For long, I was hardened by my 'achieve' world where *there ain't no such thing as a free lunch*. So, to 'receive' the free gift of God's saving grace through Jesus Christ who lived and died and arose two millennia ago seemed ludicrous. But as I was dying, both physically and spiritually, the Bible's promise of abundant life[20] and eternal life[21] became the sole desire of my ebbing life. I was finally ready to receive God's saving grace. It was finally God and me; it is ultimately God and me.

Been there, done that,
And I'm not undone;
Since I found healing—
My Healing Balm of Gilead!

---

[20] I am come that they might have life, and that they might have it more abundantly. (John 10:10b, KJV)

[21] For God so loved the world, that he gave his only begotten Son, that whosoever believeth in him should not perish, but have everlasting life. (John 3:16, KJV)

Been there, done that, but I am undone; and I need healing—the Healing Balm of Gilead.

Been there, done that, but I am undone; and I need healing—the Healing Balm of Gilead.

The Healing Balm of Gilead

6

BULLS AND BEARS

He specialised in stocks and shares. His mornings started with speculation and his evenings ended with analysis. He knew the bulls and bears like the back of his hands. He was driven—driven hard by the thrills of the market.

The unexpected happens but then the very unexpected happened. An invisible enemy crept into the city and the bear swiped its paws dramatically downwards in the market. Investors were nonplussed whether to respond to fear or to hope. Sentiments sank as the virus slammed the economy and introduced new trade barriers.

He agonised over losses and lows. His mornings started with speculation and his evenings ended with analysis. His heart palpitated in concert with the erratic movements of the market. He was driven—driven hard by the vicissitudes of the market.

Business school equipped him; the market sharpened him. He did pretty well in business school; he fared pretty well in the market. But then came the unprecedented pandemic disrupting old constants and creating new variables. Panic disrupted established equilibriums.

He devised new plans and strategies. His mornings started with speculation and his evenings ended with analysis. He saw the consumer index tumbling like a sudden torrential April downpour. He was driven— driven hard by the new *abnormal*.

The market was at sixes and sevens and bewilderment was the order of the day. The hustle and bustle of life came to a standstill. The death toll was rising and the market was falling. Well acquainted with market volatility yet not with life's fragility, he paused.

He reflected on life and pondered on death. Neither did his mornings start with speculation nor did his evenings end with analysis anymore. He realised his heartbeats are not meant to keep calibrating to the market's highs and lows. He was determined—determined to regulate the pace of his life.

He realised that it profits a man little to gain the whole world and forfeit his soul.[22] He wondered if he needed to leave his marketplace dream and do a different thing. But he felt called, called to the marketplace. And if the marketplace was his calling, if his dream be from heaven sent, he perceived that it was better to obey than sacrifice.[23]

In the intensity of a month's experience, he transitioned from being driven to being called. His mornings started with gratitude and his evenings ended with hope. His passion for numbers did not diminish, it only amplified. He was inspired—inspired that his marketplace dream was given for a purpose beyond himself.

He began to understand what his professor meant by 'the beauty of mathematics', which once eluded him. He began to see numbers like never before; he saw the numbers that went into creating things of beauty and

---

[22] For what shall it profit a man, if he shall gain the whole world, and lose his own soul? (Mark 8:36, KJV)

[23] And Samuel said, Hath the Lord as great delight in burnt offerings and sacrifices, as in obeying the voice of the Lord? Behold, to obey is better than sacrifice, and to hearken than the fat of rams. (1 Samuel 15:22, KJV)

the numbers that made beautiful symphonies. He could connect seemingly paradoxical factors together in the constantly changing global marketplace. He entered into a different realm of consciousness.

Thereon, he specialised in counting his blessings twice over. His mornings started with gratitude and his evenings ended with hope. He began to understand his place in the marketplace; he began to see the marketplace ripe for harvest.[24] He was called—called not to do a different thing, but to do things differently in the light of eternity.

So, he was in the market,
But the market was not in him;
And all his mornings started with gratitude,
All his evenings ended with hope.

---

[24] Say not ye, There are yet four months, and then cometh harvest? behold, I say unto you, Lift up your eyes, and look on the fields; for they are white already to harvest. (John 4:35, KJV)

He was called—called not to do a different thing, but to do things differently in the light of eternity. He was called—called not to do a different thing, but to do things differently in the light of eternity. He was called—called not to do a different thing, but to do things differently in the light of eternity. **He was called—called not to do a different thing, but to do things differently in the light of eternity.** He was called—called not to do a different thing, but to do things differently in the light of eternity. He was called—called not to do a different thing, but to do things differently in the light of eternity. He was called—called not to do a different thing, but to do things differently in the light of eternity. He was called—called not to do a different thing, but to do things differently in the light of eternity.

Bulls and Bears

7

THE BRIDE

With Chantilly lace I got my ivory bridal dress adorned to match the soft sheen of my Akoya pearls. Preparing for the bridal march to the Baroque tune of *Pachelbel's Canon*, I obsessed over my veil and train. I picked the loveliest pair of Emmy handcrafted shoes and chose the lily of the valley for my bouquet.

My friends rejoiced with me. My family was happy for me. In merry company, he and I waited with anticipation for the coming day in the beauty of spring.

There was beauty,
And duty came calling;
So he was ready to go.

But he worried—
What if he did not come back?
He worried—
How could he leave me behind?

There was duty,
And I urged him go;
So he went.

Afterwards I worried—
What if he did not come back?
I worried—
What will I do left behind?

I waited in a coalescing world of beauty and duty. I was surrounded with the beauty of spring but my heart was in the hospital where he was responding to the call of duty. My imagination merged with the gloomy news reports; I imagined the affliction in the hospital till I could imagine no further.

I worried by day; I wept by night. While he worked and gave his very best to the sick, I froze in my isolation. Days dragged into weeks. And the weeks dragged on. I waited through the lengthening shadows in bated breath for him to come back.

I worried on by day; I wept on by night. I kept on waiting until it ceased that Maundy Thursday evening. My phone buzzed. He was gone! I was thrusted into a stony silence and I was too numb to cry. I was displaced by a vacuum in the shape of my heart. I was ruthlessly exposed to the disintegration of my world.

Even so, in the midst of it all, a strange subtle solace crept through. Wasn't it in his giving that he died? He was loving by giving. He gave because he loved.[25] Strangely, that kind of love[26] consoled my sad, sad heart and spilled through my tears. I mourned and yet celebrated this man who truly loved. In celebrating his love, my heart revived and gravitated to *agape* love that Good Friday.

He died and I couldn't be his bride,
You died and arose, and I will be Your bride,
We will be Your bride—

---

[25] For God so loved the world, that he gave his only begotten Son, that whosoever believeth in him should not perish, but have everlasting life. (John 3:16, KJV)

[26] Greater love hath no man than this, that a man lay down his life for his friends. (John 15:13, KJV)

Clothed in fine linen, bright and pure,[27]
Complete in You, unbroken forever.

Easter dawned ever so gently and I arose from my grief with a joyous consolation tucked in my heart. I tuned in to *Song for Leslie*[28], the last musical piece he and I had listened to together at a downtown church. I spent the ensuing week consolidating all that I had of him—memories and memorabilia. I sent all the wedding invitations in his drawer that he did not have the chance to send. And they are coming, coming to the marriage supper of the Lamb![29]

---

[27] And to her was granted that she should be arrayed in fine linen, clean and white: for the fine linen is the righteousness of saints. (Revelation 19:8, KJV)

[28] Tice, Jordan. "Song for Leslie". Album: Long Story, 2008.

[29] And he saith unto me, Write, Blessed are they which are called unto the marriage supper of the Lamb. And he saith unto me, These are the true sayings of God. (Revelation 19:9, KJV)

He was loving by giving. He gave because he loved. He was loving by giving. He gave because he loved. He was loving by giving. He gave because he loved. He was loving by giving. He gave because he loved. He was loving by giving. He gave because he loved. He was loving by giving. He gave because he loved. He was loving by giving. **He was loving by giving. He gave because he loved.** He was loving by giving. He gave because he loved. He was loving by giving. He gave because he loved. He was loving by giving. He gave because he loved. He was loving by giving. He gave because he loved. He was loving by giving. He gave because he loved. He was loving by giving. He gave because he loved. He was loving by

The Bride

8

CEMETERY IN THE CITY

We wanted the cemetery out of everyday view. We were busy living and we wanted to forget death. We did not want to pass by the cemetery on our way to work; we were too busy and death was too inconvenient for our thought process. We did not want our children to pass by the cemetery on their way to school; they were too young and death was too foreboding for their tender minds. "Let's shove the cemetery to the edge of the city?" And there was a resounding yes!

There was a resounding yes and we drove the old cemetery to the edge of the city. We lauded ourselves for the clever arrangement and we employed our sophisticated planning. We re-designed our urban landscape and we breathed a sigh of relief—"Ah, the city seems much better when the *stench* of death does not interfere with the *scent* of life!" With the cemetery gone, death seemed afar or so we thought. We had managed to shove the cemetery out of sight. So out of sight, out of mind, it was.

It was out of sight and out of mind until one day the virus brought the cemetery to us, right in the middle of the city. Unacquainted with sorrow, we looked for solace. Unaccustomed with suffering, we searched for meaning. Unconversant with lamentation, we yearned for condolence. We did not know what to tell our children about the cemetery we had hidden away from view for so long. Its sudden appearance jolted their consciousness and they cried hysterically.

They cried hysterically and then buried themselves in dreadful silence. We did not know what their young minds were wrestling with. We had not schooled them about the cemetery at the edge of the city. How must they be making sense of it all? Did they feel cheated out of reality by those who had more life experiences? Would they be too scared to run around again? Would they be too scarred to dream again? Would they distance themselves from life?

Would they distance themselves from life and refuse to connect again? Their hysteria was antagonizing but their silence was agonizing. We had borne them and we could not bear to see them wither away. Perhaps the cemetery serves a purpose not only for the dead but also for the living? Perhaps we must show our children the full picture and tell them the long story by and by? Perhaps we must let our children *come* to the Lord?[30]

So, we showed our children the full picture and told them the long story by and by and brought them to the Lord. And we built a cemetery right in the middle of the city. It was a testament to our mortality, our limited time on earth, and the infinite possibilities of a life of faith. Our mortality inspired us; we stopped fooling around with petty distractions and became real in our effort to redeem time. Day after day, the cemetery reminded us of the magnificent hope of those who died believing that they will rise when the Lord will return with the *trumpet call of God*.[31] We believed that we too will be raptured

---

[30] But Jesus said, Suffer little children, and forbid them not, to come unto me: for of such is the kingdom of heaven. (Matthew 19:14, KJV)

[31] For the Lord himself shall descend from heaven with a shout, with the voice of the archangel, and with the trump of God: and the dead in Christ shall rise first: (I Thessalonians 4:16, KJV)

to be with the Lord forever[32] and we stopped mourning hopelessly.

We stopped mourning hopelessly and our children turned their faces to the sun again. The cemetery in the middle of the city became a gentle consciousness, a visible reminder of the eternity set in our hearts.[33] The city loved life but did not fear death any longer. The city laughed more, loved deeper, and accomplished more. And it was a happy city where the children knew their Saviour and ran around and dreamed without fear.

[32] Then we which are alive and remain shall be caught up together with them in the clouds, to meet the Lord in the air: and so shall we ever be with the Lord. (I Thessalonians 4:17, KJV)

[33] He hath made every thing beautiful in his time: also he hath set the world in their heart, so that no man can find out the work that God maketh from the beginning to the end. (Ecclesiastes 3:11, KJV)

The cemetery in the middle of the city became a gentle consciousness, a visible reminder of the eternity set in our hearts. The cemetery in the middle of the city became a gentle consciousness, a visible reminder of the eternity set in our hearts. **The cemetery in the middle of the city became a gentle consciousness, a visible reminder of the eternity set in our hearts.** The cemetery in the middle of the city became a gentle consciousness, a visible reminder of the eternity set in our hearts. The cemetery in the middle of the city became a gentle consciousness, a visible reminder of the eternity set in our hearts. The cemetery in the middle of the city became a gentle consciousness, a visible reminder of the eternity set in our hearts. The cemetery in the middle of the city became a gentle consciousness, a visible

Cemetery in the City

9

AN EVENING WALK

It was a brand-new day but the day felt worn and rather old, as old as me. Confined indoors, I exhausted all the books on the shelf and I read and re-read the bunch of good old hand-written letters. I had been spending nearly all of my waking hours at my desk, and my eyes grew weary and I grew tired of viewing the world from my desk. My imagination could stretch only so far and I felt an aching need to stretch my limbs. Cloistered for long, I longed for the fresh outdoors infused with sunshine and beauty. So, after forty days were over, I put my study to rest and ventured out for an evening walk.

The neighbourhood wore a sombre look, like nothing I had known for the last seventy years of living in the city. The streets were empty and uncannily quiet. I met a few solitary pedestrians and we maintained the respectful distance of six feet. The sparrows flitted about gleefully in the tree branches and a squirrel scurried merrily around the street corner. The sun shone softly, akin to the early morning suns I know.

The peach and cherry trees along the streets took me back to my boyhood days in a hilly Himalayan town. Those were happy spring days when the peach tree in the backyard would show up with blooms. I would spend my summer holidays hopping between completing my school assignments and playing in the shade of the peach tree. Too excited to wait for autumn, I would climb up the peach tree to inspect if any of the peaches was ripe yet. As for the cherry, it was a wild Himalayan variety and stood near my bedroom window with tall upright trunk and shiny leaves. It flowered around October with delightful pinkish white blossoms and I was always sad to see them wilt and wither away every year. Ah, the memories of those jolly good days remain fresh as ever!

As I ambled further down the streets, I reached the pit garden outside an old townhouse. Whoever tended it season after season presented a personal aesthetic vision nurtured with trowel and cultivator and mulch that was delightfully different every season. I was enamoured of that pit garden as it bore an eclectic look and reminded me of a wild English garden. While the other side of the street had beds of matching begonias, this little garden was a bold assertion of a different kind of beauty. Besides, the garden housed geraniums—mother's favourite flower, much cherished for being a perennial bloom.

Further along, as I reached the big garden near the river, I was greeted by pink, red, and orange azaleas. Then there were mounds of hydrangeas shrubs nestled together in a shady corner. Glistening in the evening sun, the bunch of sprightly magenta tulips looked surreal as if made of satin. My eyes feasted on the kaleidoscope of colours and my heart bathed in the freshness of growing and blooming things.

I walked around a while relishing the garden flora and then sat reclined underneath an oak tree. The serenity of the moment made me think of the pristine beauty of the Garden of Eden.[34] The very thought of it made me

---

[34] And the Lord God planted a garden eastward in Eden; and there he put the man whom he had formed. And out of the ground made the Lord God to grow every tree that is pleasant to the sight, and good for food; the tree

elated and I looked intently at the beauty surrounding me. An undeniable joy seeped in as I soaked in the beauty of the garden and I felt oh, so uplifted. Surely, there is something about beauty that inspires joy! And wasn't it one of our own poets who said, "A thing of beauty is a joy forever?"[35]

Whilst I dwelt on beauty, the sun was setting in the horizon. And as I headed home, a group of daffodils peered out from the sideways. Robert Herricks' *fair daffodils*[36] from my school days called out to me and reminded me that the *hasting day has run to the even-song.* Homeward bound, I wondered if it was my time to go along with the daffodils after having prayed together. So much beauty, such a brief and beautiful life!

---

of life also in the midst of the garden, and the tree of knowledge of good and evil. (Genesis 2:8-9, KJV)

[35] Keats, John. "Endymion." Endymion by John Keats, E. Moxon, Son and Co., 1873, p. 1.

[36] Herricks, Robert. "To Daffodils." Robert Herricks: Selected Poems, edited with an introduction by David Jesson-Dibley, Routledge, 2003, p. 74.

Surely, there is something about beauty that inspires joy! Surely, there is something about beauty that inspires joy! Surely, there is something about beauty that inspires joy! Surely, there is something about beauty that inspires joy! Surely, there is something about beauty that inspires joy! Surely, there is something about beauty that inspires joy!

Surely, there is something about beauty that inspires joy! Surely, there is something about beauty that inspires joy! Surely, there is something about beauty that inspires joy! Surely, there is something about beauty that inspires joy! Surely, there is something about beauty that inspires joy! Surely, there is something about beauty that inspires joy! Surely, there is something about beauty that inspires joy! Surely, there is something about beauty that inspires joy! Surely, there is something about

An Evening Walk

10

A BUTTERFLY

A butterfly flapped its wings and whipped up a strange wind, causing a chain reaction reverberating around the whole wide world. The world was wide yet compact, and the impact of the wind on life and living could be felt by the populace throughout the world.

The wind did not ask for permission to enter any city and it stalked people at will. It did not consider the delineation of different skin colour; it only saw the parity of the red blood colour. Everyone was susceptible to its attack, no one was discriminated against. Everyone laid exposed to the fragility of life. A butterfly flapped its wings and levelled everyone.

As the wind strode on stochastically across borders, it rushed into unsuspecting neighbourhoods. At other times, sorrow was usually afar—in a remote spot on earth where multifarious problems of sanitation and lopsided models of development existed. But the wind brought sorrow near. Sorrow was nearer than anyone thought and crept in in unsuspecting ways into clean swanky sophisticated systems. Sorrow became a personal experience; it was not a distant news any longer.

In its trail, the wind left a different share of the same sorrow for everyone and strung the world together in sorrow. As the death count spiralled up, the world was shrouded in grief at the loss of each and every inimitable expression of life. With every breath that ceased, every heart skipped a beat but each skipped uniquely. As unique individuals, none fought to be the same, all sought to be complementary. Everyone aimed for oneness in a diverse and disrupted world.

The wind blew on and no cheery *"Business as usual!"* could be heard anymore. A century-old tearoom around the corner of the street closed its doors, never to reopen again. A cherished button store shut down with housewives and couturiers alike lamenting over it. A famous hairdresser with deft hands and fine tools discovered a different view of life and left on the last Orient flight, crushing many a gentleman's hope for a good haircut after the storm settled. The simple joy of everyday living was side-tracked. The world mourned for lost business, the world mourned for a lost lifestyle.

In its mournful state, the world turned away from loving things and using people, and began to love people and use things. The world shared toilet paper and rice. Everyone practised the pause and social intimacy was at a closest distance of six feet. Everyone recognised their neighbour and learned to put on a face covering for their own and their neighbour's sake. The world started exercising its heart. The world emulated the *good Samaritan*.

Propelled by the raging wind, everyone responded to the call of duty—some through ceaseless activity, some by ceasing activity. Some stayed at work while some stayed at home. Freedom of movement was curbed for the greater common good. Everyone had freedom of choice, but none had freedom from the consequences of choice. More than ever, everyone became aware of their responsibilities as much as their rights.

"Am I my brother's keeper?"[37]
"Yes, you are your brother's keeper."[38]

Everyone became their brother's keeper. Everyone kept each other. Everyone metamorphosed into a finer version of themselves. Hand in hand, the world went far and stood poised at the threshold of the soaring twenties. And the butterfly flapped its wings once again and flew far far away, never to be seen again.

---

[37] And the Lord said unto Cain, Where is Abel thy brother? And he said, I know not: Am I my brother's keeper? (Genesis 4:9, KJV)

[38] Bear ye one another's burdens, and so fulfil the law of Christ. (Galatians 6:2, KJV)

"Am I my brother's keeper?" "Yes, you are your brother's keeper." "Am I my brother's keeper?" "Yes, you are your brother's keeper." "Am I my brother's keeper?" "Yes, you are your brother's keeper." "Am I my brother's keeper?" "Yes, you are your brother's keeper." "Am I my brother's keeper?" "Yes, you are your brother's keeper."

"Am I my brother's keeper?" "Yes, you are your brother's keeper." "Am I my brother's keeper?" "Yes, you are your brother's keeper." "Am I my brother's keeper?" "Yes, you are your brother's keeper." "Am I my brother's keeper?" "Yes, you are your brother's keeper." "Am I my brother's keeper?" "Yes, you are your brother's keeper." "Am I my brother's keeper?" "Yes, you are your brother's keeper." "Am I my brother's keeper?" "Yes, you are your brother's keeper." "Am I my brother's keeper?" "Yes, you are your brother's

A Butterfly

11

MONACHOPSIS

What does it feel like to be a square peg in a round hole? Monachopsis. It is the inherent gnawing feeling of being a misfit; the awareness of being away from your normal habitat. It is the nagging alienation of being in a place which built your fondest memories and searching for that long-lost quaint familiarity.

Monachopsis. It is the longing for a conversation when you are surrounded by deafening silence; the sigh for a dollop of vibrant colours when all you can see is grey. It is the pining for the wide expanse of blue and green when you are locked in by four red brick walls.

Monachopsis. It is the feeling of being out of your elements. It is the rift in your domain, the sense of being stripped of your essence. It is the severance from the familiar tempo of work and life, the remoteness from the exuberance of action.

Monachopsis—
It is estrangement as meaning dissipates;
It is indifference as the will to fight dissolves;
It is imbroglio as purpose disintegrates.

Monachopsis. It is when you are locked down trying to explain what is happening, struggling to understand what is going on, striving to grasp everything.

If you can explain it all, where's the mystery?
If you can understand it all, where's the mystique?
If you can grasp it all, where's the miracle?

Monachopsis. It is when you are locked down unable to explain what is happening, unable to understand what is going on, unable to grasp anything.

When you can't explain it all, think of Mystery.
When you can't understand it all, muse on Mystique.
When you can't grasp it all, allude to Miracle.

Monachopsis. It is simultaneously being dissuaded by what you see and being persuaded by what you believe. It is the persistent awareness that there is more than meets the eye. It is the subtle lingering consciousness of a greater reality than the immediate. It is ever tending to the *there and then* in the *here and now*.

Monachopsis. It is the glimmering hint of a place you have not been yet, a country[39] you have not seen yet where wisdom reigns supreme, where all the ways are pleasant and all the paths are peace.[40] You are made for this time and place and yet you are also made for that country. Your citizenship is in that heavenly country.[41] The sense of monachopsis alludes to it. And the heart knows it.

Monachopsis. Your habitat is where you are fully alive, where you are fluidly your very best self, where you realise the purpose of your being and your powers. Therein your hazy sorrow is removed, and you meet gladness of heart and love to quiet you.[42] You belong

---

[39] But now they desire a better country, that is, an heavenly: wherefore God is not ashamed to be called their God: for he hath prepared for them a city. (Hebrews 11:16, KJV)

[40] Her ways are ways of pleasantness, and all her paths are peace. (Proverbs 3:17, KJV)

[41] For our conversation is in heaven; from whence also we look for the Saviour, the Lord Jesus Christ (Philippians 3:20, KJV)

[42] The Lord thy God in the midst of thee is mighty; he will save, he will rejoice over thee with joy; he will rest in his love, he will joy over thee with

where you are kept as the apple of the eye and hidden in the shadow of the Almighty's wings.[43]

Monachopsis. You only feel out of place because there is a place where you belong.

---

singing. (Zephaniah 3:17, KJV)

[43] Keep me as the apple of the eye, hide me under the shadow of thy wings. (Psalm 17:8, KJV)

You only feel out of place because there is a place where you belong. You only feel out of place because there is a place where you belong. You only feel out of place because there is a place where you belong. You only feel out of place because there is a place where you belong. You only feel out of place because there is a place where you belong. **You only feel out of place because there is a place where you belong.** You only feel out of place because there is a place where you belong. You only feel out of place because there is a place where you belong. You only feel out of place because there is a place where you belong. You only feel out of place because there is a place where you belong. You only feel out of place because there is a place where you belong. You only feel out of place because there is a place where you

Monachopsis

12

MONDAYS OF MY LIFE

The long-awaited Monday came. The city was at work again after an unwelcome break introduced by the pandemic. As I reached my desk, I slumped into my chair with my head bowed low remembering a colleague will not be coming to work anymore.

"How now should I live? How now should I work?" Overwhelmed with the brevity and uncertainty of life, I determined to marshal every ounce of energy and be relentless in my pursuit of excellence. I worked frantically that week and I was proud to have set a new benchmark in performance. I was proud but I had no peace. Devoid thus of peace, I was unable to utter any praise.

So, I could not—
Thank God it's Monday,
Nor thank God it's Friday.

Weekend dawned. My toddler was peacefully at play, unmoved by the world around. My octogenarian father was peacefully reading the newspapers, unnerved by the news. I envied them both in equal measure. I wondered what happens to a person in the intervening years of being a child and becoming a child again.

I became a case study unto myself. I was hyperactive preparing for the worst-case scenario and priming for the best-case scenario. Glad to have survived the pandemic, I found myself full of nervous energy trying to squeeze the most out of life. Ever restless, I was spending my substance in childish ambition and missing out on childlike peace. So, I decided to slow down and learn the simplicity of being a child again. I decided to weigh my pursuit of excellence and my pursuit of peace.

That Saturday, as we gathered for the family prayer at eventide, father exhorted, "Let your zeal for excellence be sanctified". Together in worship, we contemplated on the Psalm of David: *"Lord, my heart is not haughty, nor mine eyes lofty: neither do I exercise myself in great matters, or in things too high for me. Surely I have behaved and quieted myself, as a child that is weaned of his mother: my soul is even as a weaned child."*[44]

Then came Sunday and I heard the preacher sermonise, *"As you worship, so you believe, so you live."*[45]

Sunday was peaceful, Sunday was smooth—
After all, I was in the sanctuary.

But as night fell, I began wondering, "What about the Mondays of my life? What about Tuesdays through Fridays?" I was flustered that the pursuit of peace seemed so elusive.

Seeing anxiety writ large on my face, my father said to me, "Son, remember it is written: *'Come unto me, all ye that labour and are heavy laden, and I will give you rest.'*[46]" So, I considered the call and went to the Lord as the city slept. Bent on becoming a man of peace, I knelt in prayer

---

[44] Lord, my heart is not haughty, nor mine eyes lofty: neither do I exercise myself in great matters, or in things too high for me. Surely I have behaved and quieted myself, as a child that is weaned of his mother: my soul is even as a weaned child. (Psalm 131:1-2, KJV)

[45] A motto in Christian tradition, known in Latin as *Lex Orandi, Lex Credendi, Lex Vivendi*.

[46] Come unto me, all ye that labour and are heavy laden, and I will give you rest. (Matthew 11:28, KJV)

in earnest expectation of an overnight miracle to make of me what I couldn't by myself.

Monday came and the city awoke but miracle defied my expectation. I did not experience a swift kind of miracle. But little by little, I experienced a slow movement of grace attuning my heart to worship God and syncing me into a peaceful rhythm of work and rest. I did more by resting in Him than by struggling in my own strength. I worked better having rested *in* Him, I rested better having worked *for* Him. I rested and dreamed, I worked and excelled. I experienced a steady kind of miracle— peace that surpasses all understanding.[47] And peace taught me praise.

So, I now can—
Thank God it's Monday,
And thank God it's Friday!

---

[47] And the peace of God, which passeth all understanding, shall keep your hearts and minds through Christ Jesus. (Philippians 4:7, KJV)

corona in the city . corona in
the city . corona in the city .
corona in the city . corona in
the city . corona in the city .
corona in the city . corona in
the city . corona in the city .
corona in the city . corona in
the city . corona in the city .
corona in the city . corona in
the city . corona in the city .

corona in the city . corona
in the city . corona in the
city . corona in the city .
corona in the city . corona
in the city . corona in the
city . corona in the city
corona in the city . corona
in the city . corona in the

So, I now can thank God it's Monday and thank God it's Friday! So, I now can thank God it's Monday and thank God it's Friday! So, I now can thank God it's Monday and thank God it's Friday! So, I now can thank God it's Monday and thank God it's Friday! So, I now can thank God it's Monday and thank God it's Friday! So, I now can thank God it's Monday and thank God it's Friday! So, I now can thank God it's Monday and thank

So, I now can thank God it's Monday and thank God it's Friday! So, I now can thank God it's Monday and thank God it's Friday! So, I now can thank God it's Monday and thank God it's Friday! So, I now can thank God it's Monday and thank God it's Friday! So, I now can thank God it's Monday and thank God it's Friday! So, I now can thank God it's Monday and thank God it's Friday! So, I now can thank God it's Monday and thank God it's Friday! So,

Mondays of My Life

corona in the city . corona in the
city . corona in the city . corona
in the city . corona in the city
corona in the city . corona in the
city . corona in the city . corona
in the city . corona in the city .
corona in the city . corona in the
city . corona in the city . corona

corona in the city . corona
in the city . corona in the
city . corona in the city
corona in the city . corona
in the city . corona in the
city . corona in the city
corona in the city . corona
in the city . corona in the
city . corona in the city
corona in the city . corona
in the city . corona in the

Printed in the United States
By Bookmasters